Wicked In My Own Way

Kayleigh King

ISBN:1493768131
ISBN-13: 978-1493768134

Dedicated to my beautiful wife Kerry. My life, my love, my everything.

CONTENTS

Chapter	Page Number
1	7
2	14
3	20
4	23
5	30
6	35
7	41
8	52
9	61

1

The bank was unusually busy for a Monday afternoon. Its moderately full capacity did nothing to help the already stuffy heat inside the building. Thanks to a broken air conditioning unit coupled with unusually warm weather, life was becoming very difficult for Lucy to keep her equilibrium. As a customer advisor she was supposed to maintain a happy, welcoming exterior at all times. She sighed as she brushed a stray strand of damp blonde hair out of her eyes and pushed it behind her ear. She shrugged off her blazer and hung it on the back of her chair. It did little to alleviate the cloying heat but it made her a tad more comfortable. She contemplated opening another button on her white blouse which was beginning to cling to her skin due to the thin sheen of sweat. This thought was halted by the whiff of cheap musk from over her left shoulder. She shuddered with barely concealed disgust. *Dwayne*.

Dwayne could be seen by many people as a catch. On the surface he seemed to have it all. He had money, looks and what he wrongly considered to be charm. But all Lucy could see was a materialistic, shallow creep of a man who spent more time talking to her breasts than her face. He was in all honesty, the embodiment of the type of men she avoided. Her love life had never really been anything to write home about, she'd never found anyone that had truly ignited any spark of passion within her. She could never seem to connect to anyone.

As Dwayne was her manager she was obligated to interact with him. That meant dealing with his "jokes" which usually referred to women in kitchens or bedrooms, his "compliments" which included words such as 'fuck-able' and 'hot' and worst of all his pungent albeit probably expensive after shave. She supposes he wasn't the worst kind of man but on a normal day his supposedly alluring glances and wandering touches were enough to make her want to scream, therefore in this heat she might just kill him. Far from being allured she spent most of the time torn between wanting to disinfect her body and fighting the urge to remove his genitals from the rest of his body. She felt him lean into her side as he brought his head down to her level, and fought the urge to gag.

“Hey Luce...” he drawled, his eyes trailing up and down her body. She tried yet again to tamper down her anger. She debated telling him for the hundredth that she hated the shortening of her name but opted to just let it go. No point starting a conversation she truly had no patience of even pretending to be able to tolerate.

She turned slightly in her chair, subtly angling her body away from his unappealing smell and his "sexy" facial expression. She just wanted to get her day over with, go home, take a shower and curl up with a glass of wine. Knowing she couldn't ignore him, she opted for her most uninterested expression and simply replied “Is there something you need Dwayne?” She realised far too late her mistake as his face morphed into a salacious grin and he canted his eyebrow. His propensity for turning the most innocent phrases into innuendo was gross, but also slightly impressive on some days.

“Well Luce, can you give me what I need?” he drawled. He dragged his finger up her bare arm and leant in closer. “I need to know why you won’t give me a chance. All I wanna do is take you out somewhere nice, have a nice meal, maybe some dancing. We could see where the night takes us. I could show you such a great time. Ya’know loosen you up a bit”

In a well practiced move, Lucy pulled her chair back to gain some distance. She placed her hand on his chest, effectively halting his movement as he tried to close in again.

“Dwayne, I've told you. Actually I've told you more times then I should have to. I have no interest in going anywhere with you. I just don't see you in that way, and I sure as hell don’t need ‘loosening up’. We are colleagues and nothing more.”

Letting out a short sigh, Dwayne's face softened.

“Ok ok, well I just wanted to invite you to Carlo's tonight after work. No funny business I assure you. It's Janet's leaving drinks, it should be a laugh.”

Lucy felt her heart drop. As much as she'd rather be anywhere else than in Dwayne's greasy presence, she knew she would be missed. She had worked with Janet for a few years now so she should really be there to say goodbye. Janet had been a firm friend as well as a great person to work with, almost a mentor of sorts.

“Of course I'll be there for Janet.” The ‘not for you’ was left unspoken but by the look on his face, he had received the message loud and clear.

After he slinked away, Lucy quickly collected herself as a customer approached her desk. The man was in his early to mid-fifties, with unkempt graying hair and small half moon spectacles on his head carrying what looked like a tatty vintage briefcase. As he reached her, he began patting at his pockets erratically, obviously searching for something. After locating his glasses case his look of joy soon morphed into a small frown as he opened them only to find the case empty.

Chuckling, Lucy softly stood and asked “Sir?” She barely restrained her giggle as he visibly jumped. When she had he attention, she quickly pointed to his head. His cheeks quickly reddened as his hand met the frames resting just above his hairline.

As he slid them over his eyes, he sheepishly answered a brief ‘thank you’.

Remembering herself, Lucy found that for the first time today her smile was genuine and not a job requirement. Her training kicked in as she cheerfully greeted her customer.

"Good Afternoon, my name is Lucy. What can I do for you today?" She held out her hand and he shook it firmly, he seemed to startle slightly at the touch but didn't comment. Lucy wondered if her hands were a touch sweaty. As she gestured for him to be seated, she quickly wiped her palms on her skirt.

He cleared his throat as he introduced himself,

"Hello, my name is Dr Jonah Klein and I would like to open an account. I have completed all the forms and I would like to deposit a large sum of money."

He laid the tatty case on the desk, fiddling with the combination lock before thumping his fist loudly on its side. The noise resonated throughout the entire bank and drew a lot of attention which went unnoticed by Dr Klein. The case sprang open, sending papers flying everywhere. Dr Klein deftly gathered them up and pushed them towards Lucy.

As she began smoothing out the papers, her eyes were drawn to a particular document. The form was for a pre-approved transfer from one of the world's largest banks. That wasn't the detail that caught her attention. The part what grabbed hold was the total under the line for amount. It simply read, *25 million pounds*. Dr Klein tilted his head at her dumbfounded expression.

"Is there a problem?" He asked. Lucy pulled herself together to reply.

"I apologise Dr Klein, I was just a little taken aback by the amount. I apologise for my lack of manners." He simply waved her off.

"Do not worry, my child. Maybe I should explain. I am currently in the employ of the Noble Corporation. I have been living in Canada for the past 6 years but I am now working in London and this banking establishment was recommended. As I prefer to deal with all matters myself I thought it was best I come in person to deal with things. I did initially have an appointment with a Mr Dwayne Cunningham but I was bluntly informed that he was busy. After waiting for a while I saw you were free."

Lucy understood completely what had happened. Dwayne prided himself on dealing with the more 'select' clients. One look at Dr Klein and he would have decided he had better things to do. She tapped away at her computer, bringing up a number of files she'd need to quickly fill in from the information in front of her.

After taking a copy of the Doctor's ID and inputting the first round of information she was startled by the ringing of her desk phone. A glance at the handset showed a blinking light next to Dwayne's extension. She answered as politely as she could manage.

"Hello, Lucy Blackhall's desk"

"Yea Luce hi. You need to stop what you're doing, You've just put 25 mil through the system!"

Wary of the gentleman sat opposite, Lucy kept her tone measured.

"I am aware of that transaction, Sir."

"Holy shit! This is legit? Is the client with you right now?"

Lucy smiled apologetically at Dr Klein, indicating with a finger that she'd only be a minute.

"Yes Sir, I'm right in the middle of..." She was cut off by the dial tone, indicating she had in fact been hung up on. She quickly placed the phone back, and looked back at Dr Klein. The man, who just a few moments ago was smiling kindly now had a scowl etched on his face. Before she could enquire what was wrong, a strong tap on her shoulder accompanied by a gagging cloud of cologne let her know what was going to happen next.

Dwayne stood there, all swagger and pomp. Looking just like the same prat he always did. He didn't even look at her as he began to talk.

"It's ok Lucy I can take it from here." Lucy began to collect her things as he carried on, extending his hand to be shaken.

"Mr Klein so sorry I'm late I was stuck in a meeting, my name is Dwayne Cunningham and I can help you with whatever you need today."

The older man regarded the younger man with a critical eye, making no move to shake the offered hand. Dr Klein lazily removed his spectacles and proceeded to clean them with a handkerchief he had produced from his jacket pocket.

"Mr Cunningham. Nice of you to join us, but with all due respect I am in no need of your assistance."

Dwayne pulled his hand back and stuffed it in his pocket, obviously not expecting that reaction.

"Well Mr Klein-" Dr Klein held up a hand to halt his prattling.

"Firstly, it's Dr Klein. Secondly, I saw you sat here harrassing this poor young lady well into our allotted meeting time. So please do not lie to me. Secondly, Miss Blackhall is doing a fine job of attending to my affairs so I will only be dealing with her in the future. Is that understood?"

Dwayne could do nothing but nod dumbly, his face betraying the confusion he obviously felt. His ego wasn't used to the treatment he was receiving

"Well I'll get back to my office as I am a very busy man." And with that he scurried away leaving Lucy alone once again with her new favourite customer.

"Dr Klein, are you sure you wish to deal with me? There are many employees in this building with much more experience with larger accounts such as yours. I assure any one of them would be happy to assist you." Dr Klein simply smiled as he adjusted his glasses.

"No my dear, I am perfectly sure. I am definitely sure it is YOU that I need."

2

Carlo's bar was a small, lesser known bar in the fashionable parts of Soho only a few streets away from the bank. It was a favourite of the staff as the owner was the father of the security guard, Bob. So, of course there was always room for the colleagues and with a slightly smaller than normal bill at the end. It was a rarity in London, a great place to go that wasn't packed with tourists. Bob's father Carlo was a large built Italian man whose voice could be heard over even the loudest din. His warm face and no-nonsense attitude reminded her so much of her late Grandfather that it was impossible for her to not smile in his presence. He was a bear of a man who had always welcomed her with a beaming smile and a lovingly crushing hug.

On this night as she walked into the bar, she heard her name being called in a hearty Italian accent as soon as she crossed over the threshold. All her hesitation was swept away at the embrace of the kindly man-mountain. He ushered her to a booth near the window, snatching the reserved sign from the table as he went. The sign was a habit from weekend nights to guarantee them the best table, the bar on a Monday night was only half full. He disappeared briefly behind the large wooden bar only to reappear about a minute later with a large colourful drink, complete with a little umbrella and novelty sparkler. The drink was deposited in front of her with a flourish and a wide grin. At her bemused expression he added dramatically,

"To cheer you up my Lucy! A pretty girl like you should always have a smile on her face!"

She chuckled at his remark, once again warmed by his affection. She patted his hand.

"It's just been a long day Carlo, thanks for the drink"

As she reached for her purse, he waved her off.

"This one is on me." he said softly before turning back to help behind the bar.

Great. She thought. *How pathetic must I look?* She turned to look outside where the remainders of her group were finishing their cigarettes. She had headed inside under the guise of the unnecessary act of 'grabbing a table', just so she could escape from Dwayne's presence. It may have been her imagination but today he seemed to be more, *intense* then usual. Ironically it had been since their earlier discussion where Lucy thought she had cleared the air regarding whatever misgivings he had about their 'relationship'. Though, even now he was staring at her through the window. She couldn't quite put her finger on what the difference was. He was always a creep, but today he seemed to be even more focused on her and it made a sliver of fear slide down her spine. Her reverie was broken by the arrival of her work mates. Before Dwayne could sit beside her with his ever-present cloud of pungent cologne, Lucy stood with her drink and handbag, motioning to the mass of huddled smokers outside. Each of her co-workers smiled in acknowledgement and continued with their conversations and drink orders. Of course with the exception of Dwayne. He stepped back minutely to let her pass, his hand stroking her backside as she went. His intention was all too clear. The earlier discussion had obviously fallen on deaf ears. It was clear now, he didn't misunderstand, he just doesn't care. This is a fact that Lucy isn't sure how to deal with.

In her haste to cross to the door that she sees as her brief freedom, she fails to see the firm leather-clad body in her path. As they collide, her bag tips. She watches mortified as her lighter skitters across the floor. The heat rushes to her face as she cringes, feeling arms reaching out to steady her.

"I'm so sorry I wasn't looking where I was going-" She stutters out as she fumbles to keep balanced, not wanting to cover herself or anyone in the sweet crimson drink as she pulls back. Looking up, her breath catches as she locks onto the eyes of her obstacle. The stormy brown eyes hold a wicked glint, seemingly amused and nonplussed at the same time. Lucy tries to speak but feels herself slightly at a loss of words; she's rescued briefly as the owner of the eyes crouches down smoothly then swiftly stands, coming closer to Lucy than she was before. It's now that Lucy takes in more features, the sharp dark eyebrows, the olive skin, the slender nose that leads down to full red lips. Long inky black hair that frames the face of what must be the most beautiful woman Lucy had ever seen. As she tries to ignore the unfamiliar pangs of what can only be lust, she realises she should probably either say or do something. She's saved from any more awkwardness as the woman cants an eyebrow and holds out the lost lighter.

"Sorry about that. I hope I didn't hurt you?"

The woman's voice is a surprisingly low tone with a slightly Hispanic accent. Lucy can do nothing but gently shake her head and reach for her lighter. As their fingers brush she tries to ignore the spark that works its way through her hand and up her arm. If the other woman felt anything she had a great poker face so Lucy attempted to carve herself some dignity.

"No I'm fine. Sorry. It was my fault- sorry"

Her delivery wasn't as smooth as she was hoping for and she felt herself wince. The mortification only intensified as she looks down to see she's still holding the other woman's hand. The woman in question only smiles as she squeezes Lucy's hand before releasing.

"No need to apologise quite so much. It was just an accident. Let me buy you a drink so you know there are no hard feelings?"

The woman's tone was somewhere between blasé, flirty and hopeful and Lucy wasn't quite sure what the protocol was. She pulled her bag further onto her shoulder, catching her table in her periphery. A few curious faces stared her way, watching the interaction. She was aware of the rumors at work that started when she'd knocked back the advances of the few office Casanovas. The words “lesbian” and “frigid” had rung in her ears for a month or so until they dissipated and the gossips moved on to new fodder. No-one had directly enquired, not that it was anyone's business anyway. But if they had, Lucy would have told the truth. She wasn't ashamed of her bisexuality.

A quick scan of the faces showed equal parts jealousy and intrigue from the men and curiosity and titillation from the women. She faltered when she reached Dwayne. His face was the picture of barely concealed rage. It wasn’t a look she had seen on his face before. She felt the bottom fall out of her stomach as she felt her panic rise, already concocting ways to leave as soon as possible.

As if sensing her distress the woman seemed to take pity on her. Motioning to the cigarettes still clutched in Lucy's hand she spoke,

“Why don't you answer me when you come back in? I'll be at the bar 'kay?”

Once again at a loss for words Lucy just nodded before continuing her towards the door. The wind was strong and biting, so she moved to the alley beside Carlo's. She internally rolled her eyes as she cupped a hand around a cigarette trying to coax it to stay lit. She takes a further step back, out of the path of the wind and gives a silent cheer as she successfully inhaled a hit of nicotine. She paid no mind as she heard the door open and close, people were constantly milling in and out of the warmth for their vice. That was a mistake. The wind whipped past her face again, blowing her hair into her eyes, she pushed it away and froze. That smell. She didn't even have time to focus as she felt hands push her further into the dark alley before she was unceremoniously slammed against the rough brick wall, her glass smashing on the ground. An arm pinned across her chest as a hand pressed against her mouth to quieten her. Her instinct was to struggle, but she was held with a firmness that was beyond painful.

"Now now Lucy, let's not play any more games. I know what girls like you need. You love the chase, but all it takes is a bit of attention and you are practically soaked"

He spat the words at her, sprinkling her face with foul saliva even as she tried to pull away. The moisture melded with the tears she hadn't noticed shedding, her body filling with ice-cold fear as she realised that she was alone with a man she needed to be far away from. Dwayne moved his arm from her chest, changing instead to run his palm lazily down the front of her body, brushing close to her breasts. As his fingers drew close to the button on her trousers, Lucy felt a stirring inside her. The stirring was in no way sexual. It felt like her limbs were turning to Iron, red hot liquid strength traveling through her veins as if fortifying her. Steeling herself, her eyes closed she brought her hands up in a blur of motion and pushed against the chest of her would-be attacker. He made an undignified *splat* sound as he hit the wall on the other side of the alley, his head bouncing slightly off the brick. Lucy supposed in any other situation the look of bewilderment he wore would be comical. In this situation however it was a brief flash before his face again twisted in anger. In the blink of an eye he was on her again, this time with a hand curled tightly around her throat, pressing her against the brick.

"You bitch!" He spat.

He reared his arm back and Lucy prepared for the impact, squeezing her eyes closed. However it never came. Squinting her eyes open, she saw Dwayne looking towards the entrance of the alley. Following his line of sight, she was met with the gaze of the mysterious woman from their earlier collision who was slightly smiling.

"Sorry to interrupt guys, I was hoping one of you had a light?" She held up an unlit cigarette, as if to verify her point. Lucy had yet to breathe again. She wished at this moment that she was psychic. She was screaming inside her head *Run! Go get help!*

But the woman didn't look too concerned. Lucy pleaded with her eyes as the woman stepped forward. Dwayne hadn't moved although he had loosened his grip slightly, allowing Lucy to breathe slightly. His eyes raked down the newcomer's body as if he was looking at his next meal. He glanced at Lucy before opening his vile mouth.

"We're just having a little chat aren't we babe? Just having a laugh so why don't you just piss off?"

The dark woman quirked her head in Lucy's direction and let out a quick laugh.

"Well I hate to break it to you man, but she doesn't seem to be having any fun at all. In fact it looks like the only person having fun is you."

Lucy didn't understand what was going on. It was clear that she needed help so why was the woman not helping? Why was she just stood there smirking? The answer came quickly as Dwayne had apparently run out of patience. One minute Lucy was on her feet against the wall, the next her face was bouncing off the floor where she'd been thrown then only darkness.

When she opened her eyes she was sat propped up against a cold brick wall. No Dwayne or beautiful woman in sight. Her earlier drink had splashed her when she'd dropped it. The stain was now dry and caused her blouse to stick uncomfortably to her skin. A brief look through the door showed her workmates drunkenly singing and laughing. Deciding she wouldn't be missed, she grabs her bag and makes her way to the tube station. She'd had more than enough of this shit for one night.

3

Lucy breathed in a sign of relief as she exited the station, intent on hurrying around the corner. Eager to get home. She rubbed her forehead in agitation as she climbed the stairs to her flat. It was a good size compared to some of the shoe-boxes you could end up with in London. Her Grandmother had left it to her when she'd passed, coming up to four months ago now. It had a great view of Big Ben... if you craned your neck to the left on a clear day. It was in a nice area, quite quiet but friendly. It wasn't much but it was home. Shrugging her bag to the other shoulder she thrust her key into the lock, let herself in and kicked it shut behind her. The satisfying sound of the lock clicking into place filled her with relief, giving her the first feeling of safety since Dwayne had held her against the rough wall. She was familiar enough with the layout to manoeuvre around without worrying about the lack of light. It was the red blinking light on her answering machine caught her eye. The screen informed her that she had 3 messages, which wasn't entirely unusual. The first two messages were promptly deleted as salesmen waxed lyrical as to the virtue of their products. Expecting to hear more droll tones of people trying to sell her insurance or wall insulation she came to a sudden stop as she heard the voice she wasn't prepares to hear again.

"Hi Luce it's Dwayne. I er- I just wanted to say no hard feelings about that silly little misunderstanding tonight ok? We don't need to talk about it again ok? See ya."

Blinking slowly, Lucy quickly pressed the button to replay the message. After her third listen she was still struck dumb. He had assaulted her; had tried to do something unspeakable to her, yet here he was making it sound like it was somehow a mistake. How could he call it a misunderstanding? How could he make it sound so trivial? She played the message again and felt her arms shake as the anger built. She could feel his bravado, his ego obviously not allowing him to admit that he'd tried to rape her. Well his ego and possibly the fact that he would just incriminate himself. What she couldn't understand either was the underlining of fear in his voice. Maybe he thought she'd gone to the police? In that moment she couldn't understand why she hadn't. She could have gone to Carlo and he'd have gotten her help. But she knew the answer. She'd panicked. But she would call the police. She conceded that she'd left things with the man in quite the tenuous position, because what the hell happened to him? He had been bigger and stronger, and he had tried to take advantage of that. Of course she had managed to push him off, although she was unsure how. Putting it down to an adrenaline rush seemed like the best way to avoid a headache. When the mystery woman had interrupted them it felt as though she was being saved, which she supposed she had been. Even after her little moment of fight-back, she was unsure what her next move would have been. It had been a long day and the week wasn't even close to being over. A strange feeling of guilt swept over her for a moment. It occurred to her that she didn't know what happened to the woman or to Dwayne. Had he hurt her? Had she gotten away? She had to call the police.

She'd been dreaming of a hot shower her entire journey home, squeezed into a seat next to a rather inebriated rotund man. She gently touched her breastbone, feeling the tenderness caused by Dwayne's attack. She wondered whether attack was the right word, but she quickly settled on the word. It most definitely was an attack, but she couldn't shower. The police would want evidence. She decided she get changed so it would be easier to hand over her clothes.

Starting her journey to the bathroom, she quickly unbuttoned her ruined blouse as she picked up the remote for her stereo. A few taps and the dulcet tones of Adele escaped from the discreet speakers in every room. One of the few luxuries she allowed herself. She hoped it would calm her. She crossed to the bedroom and finally flicked on a light. The high pitched squeal she emitted would have been hilarious to her if it had been anyone else making the sound. Lucy raised her hands to her heart as the warm glow illuminated the figure on her bed. The soft light contrasted sharply with the olive skinned beauty that Lucy quickly recognised. The green eyes before her sparkled with mirth as she tried to keep her obvious amusement from reaching her face. The smooth skin and strong jaw flashed through her mind as she recalled her interaction with this woman only about an hour previously. The recognition did nothing to quell the fear at the knowledge that someone was in her home, uninvited. The fear was obvious on her face as she tried to understand what her next move should be. The mysterious woman uncrossed her legs and slowly rose from where she was seated on the bed. Her hands rose quickly in a sign of surrender, hoping to convey that she wasn't a threat. The familiar smirk from earlier twitched on her lips as she spoke, but seemed to falter slightly at the woman's reaction.

“Lucy, please don't be scared. I'm not going to hurt you I just need to talk to you.” The dark woman’s eyes seemed to almost plead. The blonde was speechless. A blizzard of thoughts stormed through her brain as she tried to work out what to do, whether fight or flight was the best option. A chill on her stomach reminded her that she was currently half naked. Her hands flew to her buttons, fastening them haphazardly as she stumbled slightly backwards out of the room. In her haste her feet caught in her the straps of her discarded handbag. The last thing she remembered was falling backwards before the world went dark for the second time that night.

4

The pain was what she noticed first. It radiated from the back of her skull where it settled and throbbed between her temples. The second was the sensation of what she deciphered to be soft fingers stroking along her forehead, then through her hair. She cracked an eye open slowly, wincing as the light from a lamp sparked white heat through her hand. At her movement the hand settled firmly on her shoulder pushing her to recline again. Her body tensed as the memory of Dwayne's rough treatment pushed itself to the forefront of her brain, and cold terror flooded her system. The dark beauty beside her cursed herself as she realised the situation. She released her grip and hastened to explain herself.

"Lucy please calm down. My name is Kyra. I am sorry for this. I truly never meant to scare you and I promise I mean you no harm. Please just let me explain."The realisation came quickly that the person hovering above, was not her would-be attacker, but the woman who had aided her. This calmed her, albeit briefly. She also remembered the woman had been lying in wait for her... and somehow knew her name and address. The thought occurred that if the woman truly meant her harm she had had more than enough opportunities tonight, hell she'd been bloody unconscious. She kept her eyes closed as she pushed herself up to a seated position, trying not to tense at the soft grip at her elbow helping her. Slowly Lucy opened her eyes again, gratefully noting that the lamp had been angled away from her face. Her unbidden first thought was that the woman was even more beautiful in this light. She brought her hands up to scrub her face, the fingers of her right hand trailed over the plaster that had been applied to the cut above her eyebrow from her encounter with the pavement earlier.

"I took the opportunity to clean your cut whilst you were

unconcious. Sorry but it looked a little red. Fortunately there's just a bump to the back of your head it didn't break the skin. I also put a t-shirt on you." The voice startled her. Lucy wasn't sure how to reply to- *wait what's her name? Kerry? Kara? No wait Kyra.* Looking to her left she looks into brown eyes and steels her resolve, noticing quickly that she herself was now fully clothed.

"It's Kyra right?" She asked trying to keep the tremor from her voice. At the woman's relieved nod she carried on.

"I don't mean to be rude, I really don't. But what the hell are you doing in my home? How do you know where I live? How do you know my name? AND what the fuck happened earlier with Dwayne?" Kyra leant forward, elbows resting in her knees. Amused, she ran her fingers through her hair then waggled them in front of her.

"Well to answer your question, I'm here for you. I wanted to make you're ok after what happened earlier and I needed to make sure you're ok. The second question is a bit of a long story. My father knew your parents, they were old friends."

"Wait what? What do my parents have to do with this? They died twenty years ago!" Lucy was immediately defensive. She really didn't want to think about that time in her life. Thinking about the time you were 5 years old and watching your home burn with your parents in it doesn't really appeal. Kyra remained silent at the look of pain in Lucy's eyes. This isn't what she wanted, but it was an opening none the less. There was so much that needed to be said. She tried a slightly different tact.

"What do you remember about them? About who they were?" Lucy shrugged off the hand still on her arm and stood abruptly.

"No. Stop asking questions! You haven't even answered mine! Why are you here?!" Lucy began to pace at a frantic pace, which quickly unsettled Kyra. She rose and placed herself in Lucy's path, effectively stopping the blonde in her tracks.

"I will explain everything. You won't believe me but please don't stop me until I get through everything ok?" Lucy was very tempted to tell her *hell no* and call the police but something stopped her.

"You've got 5 minutes." Kyra quickly nodded and gestured for her to take a seat but remained standing herself.

"This all goes back such a long time, Lucy. So I can only tell you so much. Our families are different. We're not like everyone else. We're faster, stronger and much more resilient. Have you never noticed that you hardly ever get ill? No broken bones? Not even as a child?" She watched as Lucy seemed to try to process what was being said. She quickly carried on.

"There are 12 families throughout the world that are the same kind, there are branches of these obviously but each person descends from a specific clan. Some clans are large with many members, such as mine. Then there are those that are smaller. In each family there is a member that makes up the council. My father was one such member. He's gone now." There was no mistaking the look in her eyes. The look spoke of a loss that Lucy pretended she could no longer remember.

"My father was known as a *Clero* a sort of historian and record keeper for our people. As his first born, I am due to take his place on the council. I was sorting out his papers, and I found several things that didn't make sense."

Against her better judgment Lucy found herself interested in this woman's story, and urged her to continue. Best to keep her distracted while she searched for her phone to call the police, because beautiful or not this woman was certifiably insane. Seeing that she still held a captive audience Kyra continued.

"I found pictures of a little blonde girl and her family, with my family at our home. I found newspaper clippings about a fire. A fire that took the lives of an entire family, the mother, father, their little girl and her Grandmother. I found legal papers that showed my Dad bought this flat then signed it over to a Mona Black. A Mona Black who became Mona Blackhall. I think she was your Grandmother and you was that little girl."

Lucy had had enough now. She stood and stepped forwards.

"Right I don't know who put you up to this but it isn't funny, at all. My Grandmother bought this flat. She never had the name Black, you're mistaken. And I died? What am I a fucking ghost? My parents died and you think it's a joke. I need you to leave right now." She gestured to the door then reached for the phone.

"Get out. I'm calling the police." She couldn't explain what happened next. One moment she was holding the phone, the next Kyra was beside her with the phone in her hands.

"Please Lucy! Just let me try to explain! I don't think you're a ghost for Christ sake! I know what you are. You are just like me! We are Doku! We're not ghosts or aliens or fucking vampires and werewolves. This isn't god dam Twilight!"

Lucy couldn't move. The air was growing hotter as Kyra got louder. It must have been the head injuries because she could swear that Kyra's eyes began to glow. The fear must have been clear as day because suddenly Kyra calmed herself. The dark woman rubbed her eyes and took a deep breath.

"This isn't working! I should have let Jonah do this!" Lucy perked up at this and narrowed her eyes.

"Jonah? Jonah Klein? He was in the bank where I work today. You know him?" Kyra managed to look at least a little bit guilty.

"Jonah works for me. I sent him to you to check you out. I needed to be sure."

"Be sure of what?"

"Sure that you were one of us." Something occurred to Lucy.

"He works for the Noble Corporation." Kyra looked perplexed at the statement.

"Er yes. I don't see your point?" Lucy rolled her eyes.

"So you work for the Noble Corporation too?" This time it was Kyra who rolled her eyes.

"No. I own the Noble Corporation. Well 17% anyway. My name is Kyra Noble." Lucy couldn't help but let her mind wander to the fact that the moment was beautiful and insanely rich. *Emphasis on the insane part.*

"We're getting off track Lucy. Maybe I should have led with this, but I found this envelope in with my father's things." She produced an envelope from inside her jacket and gently placed it in Lucy's hand. The envelope seemed old. Lucy held her breathe as she recognised her name written in her Grandmother's handwriting. As she turned it over she noticed it was closed with a blue wax seal. The seal depicted a triangular shaped symbol with strange markings around the outside.

"It's the mark of the 13th family. The family that the council believed was lost in that fire. You don't have to tell me what's in there but there is one final thing we have to talk about, but I think you need to read that before anything else."

Lucy slumped on the sofa. This was from her Grandmother. *Her Granny*. She'd know that writing anywhere. Growing up there'd been notes left on the fridge telling her how much she was loved, shopping lists not to mention letters back and forth when she was at University. She opened it and began to read.

My Dearest Lulu,

If you are reading this, then I am truly sorry because I must be gone. I am sorry because there are so many things I haven't told you and I may have left you unprepared. I don't even know where to begin. If you have this letter then I can take solace in the fact that you have the support of the Noble family. Their clan has been allied with ours for centuries. I will allow them to explain our origin and our history, for it will take some time. You may have figured out by now that the fire that took your parents was no accident. There had been talk of corruption and a brewing within our people. Your father, my son was tasked with investigating these matters and finding the answers that were needed. He had reason to believe that a single family had been instigating attacks on the humans We have lived in harmony with the humans for centuries. Human and Doku side by side. For you must know now that is what you are. With the help of Raymond Noble, we moved to London and began a new life. We would not have been safe if we had remained in Chester. That night I barely made it out of the fire alive, but you my darling were magnificent. You used your abilities to lead me to safety and you did it all at such a young age. I believe your parents were drugged before the fire was started. There is no way they would not put up a fight, and with your safety on the line I assure you they would have won. I had hoped to find a time to tell you everything as you grew older but I could not bring myself to. So I suppressed your abilities, if I am no longer around I imagine they are now becoming known to you. You now have a choice. You can suppress your abilities and live a normal life or you can choose to be trained, arrangements have been put in place to facilitate whatever decision you make. Raymond will guide and train you in secret and if you wish you can take your rightful place on the council. I do not mean to scare you my child but the fire that claimed your parents was intended to kill us all, so I must warn you that you are in danger. I have fought hard to keep you safe but there may come a time when that is not enough. Instructions have been left with Raymond, he has always been a trusted ally He will take you to a wise man, Dr Klein. He can help you. You don't remember much from your childhood, that is my doing and yet again

I am sorry. We, as a family spent many summers at the Noble home in Somerset. You were such good friends with his little girl. I implore you to think this decision through but do not wait too long. I love you my darling and please be safe.

Love Granny

P.S. Sim am adhersi ata ta

Lucy didn't realise when she had begun to cry, but as the tears dropped onto the page she realised she couldn't stop. The clang of a spoon in a cup jolted her from her misery and confusion. She looked across to the kitchen as the woman who had invaded her life emerged, holding two cups of steaming tea.

"I hope you don't mind but it looks like you need a drink and I don't think whiskey is advisable, as much as I think we'd both prefer it." Lucy took the proffered cup. Long moments passed, the only sounds being the odd slurp of a sip of tea. Lucy broke the silence by whispering.

"It's true isn't it? I'm different? And someone- someone killed my family! Oh my god did someone kill my Gran?!"

"No Lucy, I checked the hospital records, Mona died of natural causes I promise you. My father had a copy as well so I know he had checked as well. But yes, you are different but there are many of us and I can answer any questions you have. And we will find whoever killed your parents." The venom in the last phrase made Lucy look up.

"And why do you care so much who killed my parents?"

"Many reasons, the most important being that I think the same person killed my father.".

5

“I saw in the paper about your father. It was a helicopter crash right? Bad weather?” Kyra nodded and leant back into the sofa.

“That’s the official story. What actually happened is that someone tampered with the rotor blade. The helicopter took off but couldn’t maintain lift so it crashed straight down again. Dad was in there alone and he fought for control long enough to make sure no one else got hurt.”

“Sounds like a great guy.”

“He was. It’s barely been a month but there’s still a moment every morning when I wake up and forget he’s gone.” Lucy’s hand hovered above the upset woman’s knee, but she couldn’t bring herself to make contact.

“So he’s the reason that I’m still alive it seems. I should be grateful for that, and I am believe me but this is all too much. I’m supposed to make a decision. How can I? I barely understand any of this.” She kept her head down as she stared at the ground, minutely aware of the movement beside her. Kyra placed her cup on the coffee table and lifted the blonde’s chin so she was looking straight into her eyes.

“I can only give you the truth. Ask me anything you want and I’ll answer.” The close proximity once again messed with her brain, so Lucy blurted out the first question that crossed her mind.

“Can I do that glowy eye thing?” Kyra couldn’t stop the guffaw even if she wanted to.

“I said you can ask me anything and you go with THAT? Well in theory yes. You’ve been on strong doses of Blinken tea for a long time from what I can tell so it won’t come as easily as it does to me but in time, with training you can transform and do the ‘glowy eye thing' as well." Lucy thought that the air quotes were entirely unnecessary

"Blinken tea? What's that? I've never had it."

"You have. It's in the tin in the cupboard marked 'breakfast blend'. Your Granny was a cunning old bird. I bet you drink a cup every morning." The smirk on her face was as annoying as it was sexy.

"Well yeah actually. I have done for as long as I can remember. It was always our little ritual. Even at University I did. I just got used to it I suppose. Is the tea the thing that stops me being a Doku thing?" Lucy winced as she heard the words come out of her mouth. They seemed to sting Kyra for a moment, but she kept it out of her voice as she replied.

"You are not a thing. You are a Doku. Technically, we are a different subset of humans. The legend goes that in ancient times, many millenia ago, many Gods ruled the Earth. One God in particular called Dokun had a soft spot for humans and mated with many of them, and I mean a lot. The guy was a randy bastard. Anyway, the thousands of resulting children were named the Doku. They had his speed, strength and resilience but not his immortality. It's said that these Doku grew up to breed with other Doku bla bla bla and boom! There's loads of us. Not as many as there was since there was a huge war in 18th century which left only 13 of the original 21 families intact. Don't worry the 13 families were the good guys so to speak. The other 8 families wanted to rule the world, I kid you not. They wanted to wipe out the humans and take the land."

"So the Doku don't want to rule now?" She couldn't believe how crazy she sounded. Kyra huffed.

"God no! We just want to live our lives. Like I said we're not immortal. We're strong and everything but the humans greatly outnumber us. They realise who and what we are and they would hunt each and every one of us down. People are afraid of what they don't understand. Though there are some Doku who believe that Doku and humans shouldn't breed, as it sorta dilutes the stock for a lack of a better term. See me, I'm a hybrid. Half human, half Doku so I have my abilities but I have a lot of training to harness them. You, from what I could gather from my father's record are a full Doku, but with all that friggin tea you're basically human. The physiology is basically the same, for example Doku and human DNA is essentially the same. The source of our abilities cannot be found, it just IS. We see it as a kind of life force."

"So if you cut me open-"

"You'd look just like a human. All the same bits and pieces, all in the same places." Lucy thought back to what was in her letter.

"My Grandmother said I had to make a choice."

"I'm guessing the choice is whether to basically suppress your abilities or to hone them?" Lucy nodded in answer.

"Is that what we had to discuss?" At that question Kyra looked even guiltier than before.

"Actually no. What we need to discuss is the very real possibility that your life is in danger. I found you quite easily, so assuming that the person responsible for my father's death knows your alive, you may well be a target. I want you to come with me, back to Somerset to my estate. I can keep you safe while you make your decision. If you choose to keep your nature hidden I can make sure you get what you need with a new identity anywhere you like with enough money to live out the rest of your days. Or if you choose to walk this path I can make sure you get the training you need. I'm not gonna sugarcoat it, I intend to find the bastard that killed my father and haul them before the council. Then I'm probably going to rip his their head off."

"So this is like a Matrix situation? Don't I get any time to decide?"

"Yup definitely a blue pill red pill situation, girl. But the problem with time is that I don't know how long I can give you whilst keeping you safe. I took a chance engaging with you tonight. I was meant to merely observe but when that bastard put his hands on you tonight I couldn't stop myself." At the mention of the incident with Dwayne, Lucy started.

"What happened with Dwayne? I woke up and both of you were gone." Kyra at least had the good grace to look sheepish.

"Yeah sorry about that. After he threw you to the ground I kinda went all 'glowy eyed' as you call it, on him. He almost wet himself. I knocked him out and put him in Jonah's car so he could take him home. When I got back to the alley you were gone, so I got on my motorbike and headed here. You know the rest."

"Thank you for saving me." Lucy whispered, not sure what else she should say.

"Don't worry about it, and don't worry about him doing it to anyone else. I think I scared him for a good long while, and I'm going to call in a favour or two to keep an eye on him."

Before the conversation could continue a shrill ringtone blared from Kyra's jacket pocket.

"Please excuse me a moment. That's gotta be Jonah." She fumbled for her phone before jamming it next to her ear.

"Hey Jonah. What's going on?" Her olive skin paled as her eyes darted around the room.

"Right down in 2. Have the engine running." With that she slammed her phone into her pocket and looked to Lucy.

"There's no time, you have to come with me. You have 1 minute to grab anything you want to keep them we have to go."

"What! What happened to my choice?!"

"Each option began this way! Either way you would be leaving here tonight!" Lucy stood angrily, pushing herself into Kyra's space.

"Fuck you! This is my home! I'm not going anywhere!" Before she could move back Kyra had grabbed her face, a hand holding each side firmly but not painful at all.

"Lucy there are people on their way here. They are coming for you. If you stay they will kill you. I can't allow that. Please, I know you don't know me but please trust me. We need to go. NOW." There was no time for any further argument as a heavy banging started on the door. Each bang echoed around the room as both women's hearts seemed to stop for a moment. Before Lucy could move Kyra placed a hand over her mouth and signaled for her to be quiet. Taking out her phone she tapped a few keys then leant towards Lucy and whispered gently.

"Behind the sofa. Stay down and when I tell you to move you move. Right?" Lucy quickly nodded her assent and crouched behind her sofa, she briefly wondered where her blind faith had come from. As soon as Kyra saw she was safe a brief smile settled on her lips. With one last glance at Lucy she held up her phone.

"Here we go."

A button was pressed and the room descended into chaos as the door exploded into splinters, grunts of pain echoing through a now spoilt home.

6

Her ears were ringing from the blast. Her sight blurry from the flash. She shook her head, dislodging the dust and debris that had made itself home on her. It was faint at first. She thought she heard something through the ringing. Then louder. She raised her head to see Kyra's concerned face swim into view. She knew then what she heard was her name.

"Lucy! Lucy we need to move now. Watch your step but follow me now. Come on!" Lucy felt herself dragged to her feet; the sharp nicks on her soles reminded her that her feet were still bare. Followed quickly by the strange notion of how she must look. In tailored work trousers, a baggy t-shirt and bare feet. *Oh yea, definitely the look of a powerful being!*

Kyra kicked herself. She should have done all this quicker, got Lucy prepared. Bloody beautiful woman always slowed her down. She pulled the gun from the discreet holster resting at the small of her back. There was the possibility that she would have to fight her way out of here. Normally that wouldn't be a problem. But carrying a dazed woman was bound to hamper her skills a bit. She slung Lucy's arm around her shoulder, urging the woman to cling on. She lifted and moved. They had to go. She half carried Lucy across the room, easily supporting her weight with one arm. She took care to bypass the glass, wood, plaster and the few unconscious men. Small patches of fire burned but Kyra didn't seem to care.They had just reached the threshold when a man the size of a mountain blocked their way. He wore a simple black suit with a strange red symbol on his lapel. Lucy's eyes widened as she took in the size of the behemoth. Kyra seemed less concerned. He stepped forward and Kyra raised her gun and spoke in a strong, clear manner,

"I am Kyra Noble of the 12th family of Doku. State your name and affiliation."

When the man did not speak, Kyra moved her thumb and pulled the hammer of her pistol back with an audible click.

"State your affiliation or I will shoot!" The man seemed nonplussed, and Kyra was concerned that this was costing them precious time. The man lunged forward and made a grab for Lucy. His effort was met with a swift kick to his ribcage, courtesy of Kyra. The force threw his over the threshold and into the wall behind him. He slid to the floor out cold. Plaster cracks and blood evidence as to where he had impacted.

As they reached the top of the stairs Lucy had begun to regain some equilibrium. They rushed down the stairs, reaching the bottom just as the main door opened. Kyra pulled Lucy behind her and raised her gun in quick motion that served to make the blonde ridiculously dizzy. The sigh Kyra emitted was supposed to be quiet but Lucy heard it, peering around her shoulder she saw the man she had met earlier in the day. Kyra grabbed her hand and pulled Lucy forward.

"Jonah. Get her into the car; we need to get a move on. I don't want anyone waking up and seeing us leave. The neighbours are going to be a problem as well. All taken care of outside?" Jonah answered quickly.

"Yes Maam. I incapacitated three on my way in; I assume they were the second wave. Miss Lucy please come with me." For the first time, Lucy put up no resistance. As crazy as it all still seemed, there was nothing else she could do. Her home was destroyed, she was apparently not technically human and she had no idea of what would happen next. Jonah sat her in the large Bentley and fastened her seat belt. Kyra climbing in beside her briefly.

"Lucy I will be right behind you both ok? Jonah will take care of you. As stupid as it sounds, please do not be afraid." And just like that, the door was closed, and Jonah drove off. The car sped up considerably and begun it's way through Westminster.

The roar of a motorcycle behind them signaled Kyra's presence. Lucy thought of speaking to the man who was driving but she wasn't sure what was appropriate. She was exhausted and overwhelmed. She felt eyes on her, and met Jonah's eyes through the rearview mirror.

"Miss Lucy you should get some rest. We will be at the compound in a few hours."

"Compound?" Lucy couldn't remember if Kyra had mentioned this.

"Yes. The old Noble Estate. It has been fortified for your protection. You will be safe there." Lucy looked down at herself. She made a decision.

"Dr Klein?" At the sound of his title he smiled.

"You may call me Jonah, Miss Lucy." She wrinkled her nose.

"Then you at least have to call me Lucy." He smiled warmly.

"Yes Lucy?" She tensed briefly.

"Before I try to sleep could you please send a message to Kyra?" He nodded and pressed a button on the dashboard. Lucy was impressed when a screen and keyboard unfolded. He waited expectantly, his fingers poised over the keys.

"Tell her- Tell her that I choose the red pill? She'll know what it means." He furrowed his brow but typed away. At his confirmation that the message had been received, Lucy allowed her eyes to close, and let sleep claim her. Unbeknownst to the slightly slumbering woman, Kyra was smiling despite evening they'd just shared.

I knew you had it in you Lucy

After 2 hours on the road, Jonah pulled up to a large iron gate.

Pushing a hidden button on his dashboard the gate swung open allowing the car and motorbike entrance before clanging shut behind them. The road in front was in actuality the entrance to the driveway. After a minute or so Jonah brought the car to a gentle stop outside the beautiful manor house. It had been in the Noble family for generations, and right now it belonged to Kyra. Her mother lived in a penthouse in London and her brothers no longer lived at home. She had adapted it to her needs, with separate training space, including a gym, armoury, two storey garage and a large outside assault course. She was definitely getting ready for battle.

The car stopped and he looked in the rearview mirror at his passenger. Lucy was still sound asleep. He couldn't bring himself to wake her when she looked so peaceful so he awaited instructions instead. Kyra killed her engine and rolled to a stop beside the car. After removing her helmet Kyra dismounted her pride and joy the honda shadow had been the last present she had received from her father. All 1200cc of it.

"We'll need to secure the vehicles immediately." Jonah nodded and held out his hand for the keys to the bike. At Kyra's pointed look, he continued.

"Miss Blackhall is asleep, and I assume she'll be groggy upon waking. After all she has just endured maybe she'll take better to you waking her than me. I shall secure your bike then return and secure the car."

"Good thinking Jonah." She threw the keys towards the man who caught them deftly. She opened the car door as quietly as she could manage. Sitting beside Lucy, she was struck by how truly beautiful the little girl she had known had become. She quickly undid the seat belt trying not to laugh as Lucy slumped a little further towards her.

"Lucy. Lucy we're here. It's cold, we should get inside." Lucy made no move at all, still held in a deep sleep. Not knowing what to do,

Kyra gently brushed a strand of the blonde's hair out of her face being careful to avoid the injury that stood out on her forehead. Anger gripped the Latina as she remembered the incident from earlier. She had followed Dwayne on instinct; the way he had stared at Lucy made her blood boil. She hadn't been honest when she'd told Lucy that she'd knocked him out. Well she had been honest, just not completely. She'd knocked him out after breaking his nose, his leg and at least three of his ribs. Lucy's semi-conscious moans of pain had stopped her from continuing. Jonah had not been pleased when he'd been summoned to drop the unconscious man off at the nearest hospital. She had only been gone for 5 minutes but when she'd returned, Lucy had gone.

Deciding to take the path of least resistance, Kyra gently eased the smaller woman into her arms. At that moment Jonah reappeared and hurriedly unlocked the front door.

"Maam? Would you like me to take her?"

Kyra looked down at the woman in her arms and shook her head.

"No. Thanks though. I've got her."

After settling Lucy in the nearest guest bedroom, Kyra returned to the hallway. She was tired, and more than a little frazzled. She jumped when a tumbler of amber liquid was pressed into her hand.

"I thought it would calm you, Maam." Kyra downed the drink in one before placing the glass on a nearby sideboard. She wiped her mouth on the back of her sleeve before speaking.

"Why do you never call me Kyra? It's always Maam or miss. You've known me practically my whole life and now I'm older you don't use my name anymore." He looked as if he was contemplating the answer.

"I knew your father a long time. Your mother too, obviously. I saw you grow. Little Kyra who would run off and climb a tree and have us all worried for hours. When you were that age it was part of my job to protect you. And now I see it as the same. I use Maam or miss to separate the fact that you are no longer a child, because if I didn't… things would be different. For instance, tonight you would never have gone in alone. I need to separate the fact that out there 'in the field' as you love to call it you are my employer and not family. I need to be able to think about what needs to be done."

"So you don't say my name because it makes you care too much?" He rolled his eyes

"Something like that. Now Kyra, I think it's time for bed we have a busy time in front of us." Kyra smile softly as her name, and in a moment of emotion she kissed his stubbly cheek.

"Goodnight Jonah. See you in the morning"

7

Lucy breathed in deeply, feeling the air fill her lungs. As her eyes closed, Kyra's words repeated through her mind. *Focus. Strike. Block. Glide. Just breathe...*

She thought about how her life had changed so much in such a short space of time.

They had been at the compound for just over a week now. Her time had been split between reading dusty tomes with Jonah as he flitted between the old lore of her kind and his newer scientific discoveries. She smiled when she thought of the older, portly gentleman. He was a gruff man, but the kindness still shone through the grumpy exterior. He had spent a great deal of time showing her a myriad of weapons. They ranged from strange curved knives, to machine guns all the way to a sword that looked like it had been stolen from King Arthur himself. It had all made her ridiculously uncomfortable but Jonah had simply told her that her training would show her what to do.

She came to enjoy the time spent with him; he was kind and patient and took the time to help her adjust. Her physical training on the other hand was not so enjoyable. Kyra was unrelenting. Each day began with a 5 mile run, which Kyra completed without breaking a sweat whilst Lucy always ended up on the floor a sweaty hurting mess. Each day was becoming easier, as the tea left her system she felt things she had never felt before. An awareness of herself she had been missing.

After breakfast was time usually spent with Jonah, with lunch being followed almost always with what Kyra called "lingut" which Jonah had explained was Doku physical training. He explained that the training was mandatory within their people with children beginning at the age of 15, while most learn other skills even before this age. Lucy had become speechless when she saw that room for the first time. The gym was a huge room filled with a mixture of the latest hi-tech equipment and items that had definitely seen better days, such as large bags and items that seemed like an odd mixture of leather straps and metal links. The smile that had graced Kyra's face when Lucy had enquired as to the use of some of the more obscure items had definitely been devious in nature. By far her largest sources of discomfort had been the sparring and fight training. Kyra put her through her paces quickly, constantly reminding her of what she was and how she needed to learn to "find her balance". Kyra had informed her that soon they would begin grappling. Lucy was torn between anticipation and fear after hearing that little piece of information. After the brief touches they had shared, any physical contact made her body sing. It was distracting in a way she could not comprehend. Now was not the time to deal with unresolved sexual tension, as much as her body ached for it. She could see in Kyra's eyes that she felt the same. Many a time she had seen the dark beauty's eyes slip down her form.

The area they sparred in was triangular in shape, each side 10ft in length. Kyra had explained that it was an authentic Doku "Kiji" and that it should be treated with respect. It was now in the Kiji that Lucy stood. She had gravitated there after Jonah had told her to take some time to herself. She had felt drawn here. She had yet to turn like Kyra could. On a whim Kyra could transform. Although the only physical change was the glow of the eyes, Lucy swore she had felt the energy air in her living room change the first time she'd seen it. Bringing herself back to the present, Lucy continued.

She rocked back on her heels then pushed forward onto the balls of her feet, centering herself with the ground and the air around her. She was becoming familiar with the sensations that signaled the start of her transformation. She felt the blood heat as it swam through her veins, felt her nostrils flare as scents flew around her. The scent of sweat and leather mingled. She focused on what she now knew, there was no need to fight. The being inside her, WAS her, just another aspect. Another facet of herself. A facet to be embraced not fought. Lucy slowly released her breath through her mouth as she widened her stance. She yet again felt the block, she could go no further. It was almost as if she was paralysed. She tried a new approach. She brought her arms up; in front of her body following the slow flowing movements Kyra had shown her earlier. Kyra has emphasized a lot of her teachings on balance, both for Lucy's mind and body. Lucy waited for the moment that had been described to her in great detail, the moment where both psyches became one, the moment where her body housed the strongest features of both sides.

She knew what had been holding her back. Fear. The fear of losing control. The fear of accepting that it all was true, but the knowledge of the truth hadn't helped her any. Kyra had spent endless hours showing her meditation techniques and many methods of relaxation.

She was broken from her reverie by the clearing of a throat. Her eyes snapped open and locked on the object of her thoughts leaning against the door frame. She supposed she'd never get used to the woman sneaking up on her. It seemed just lately that Lucy could summon her with a single thought. Kyra straightened up to her full height and took a few steps forward.

"Penny for your thoughts?" she asked, her voice low. Lucy flexed her fingers and nervously brushed her hands down her front, conscious that she was only clad in a purple sports bra and a pair of black tracksuit bottoms, slightly less then she usually wore. It seemed like the woman was always finding her half naked. She shifted uncomfortably under the woman's gaze, as a bead of sweat ran down her spine. She never failed to feel exposed. She wasn't sure if it was from the days training or if it was just yet another effect of the beautiful woman's presence.

"My thoughts really aren't worth that much. I'm just trying to get a hold of things. I can feel the build up but I can't quite-" Her face flushed as she fumbled for the right word.

"You can't quite.......... finish?" Kyra supplied, a hint of teasing in her tone. Lucy nodded, once again marveling at the woman's skill for making everything sound sinful.

Kyra took a few more steps forward until she was less than a foot in front of her. It was only then that Lucy noticed that Kyra too was wearing training clothes. Her ensemble consisted of navy blue tank top and matching board shorts. She swallowed quickly, trying to bring her thoughts under control. Lucy could feel Kyra's eyes as they traced up her body, almost burning as she felt her eyes linger on her exposed abdomen. When Kyra's eyes finally met hers Lucy was sure she was going to pass out. The woman always had a way of turning up the temperature on any given situation. She had acknowledged her beauty, had even took the time to admit to herself that her attraction to the woman was growing. But after days and days of touching, she felt the effects ten-fold. Kyra quickly took a step back and adjusted her stance, before Lucy had a chance to query the move she ducked to avoid the spin kick Kyra aimed at her. Lucy stood her ground.

"What the hell are you doing?" She spluttered out. Kyra simply grinned as she advanced with a sideways kick perfectly followed by two swinging punches. Lucy effortlessly blocked each move but was quickly losing ground as well as her patience. Kyra simply smiled but didn't relax her posture as she spoke.

"Want to know where you're going wrong? You're thinking too much. That's your human side. You're trying to think of ways to make both sides fit together, to make them coalesce when it isn't logical."

"So what am I supposed to do? You said I had to find a balance and I'm trying!" Lucy huffed, trying unsuccessfully not to pout.

Kyra smiled indulgently, she remembered a time during her

training when she felt the same level of frustration. Although as a woman who followed her heart more than her head, she'd clicked a little earlier than the woman in front of her. She had also started her training at the age of 15 though, so her foundation was much stronger.

"You're trying to think it through. Trying to give each side equal footing, right?" At Lucy's nod she continued. "But that's the problem the balance is always changing, its fluid. There's not a switch to bring out your Doku side, the human side you're trying to find isn't there, it's a lie. Lucy, you are never just one or the other, 24 hours a day you are Doku. The only thing that changes is how much of your power you tap into. Did you even notice what you just did?"

Lucy looked confused for a moment then her eyes widened as it dawned on her. She had blocked all Kyra's moves, without thought. Kyra was still undoubtedly a better fighter which would probably always be the case, but only a few days ago Lucy had been spending all their sparring time split between hiding her face and falling on her arse.

It was then that she felt it. The almost undetectable hum in her heart. As she focused she became aware that that same hum resonated from her chest and out towards her fingers and toes. She watched her hands as she flexed her fingers, in awe of the power she could feel beneath her skin. It was slightly familiar from when Dwayne had grabbed her, but it was much easier to recognise now. She bounced lightly on the balls of her feet and was gratified at the height she reached. She felt different but altogether familiar. Her eyes snapped to Kyra's and almost gasped at the blue glow she was met with. She closed her eyes, took a deep breath and focused on letting the feeling run through her body, she felt the dam burst. When she opened them again it was Kyra's turn to gasp. Lucy knew that this time her eyes returned the glow. Without a single thought she allowed her body motion, intent on some sort of satisfaction. She glided forward and aimed a kick at Kyra's abdomen. Kyra blocked with a knee and struck out with a right hook which Lucy easily grabbed. They sparred for a while, Kyra becoming more and more impressed at how Lucy was keeping up. She speeded up and raised the intensity of her strikes. She matched each move with one of her own and after a while they were both panting from the exertion. Kyra saw her moment and flipped Lucy over her hip, landing Lucy with her back to the floor. Lucy instinctively held her own and using her momentum, flipped Kyra over her shoulders and rolled. Lucy's moment of triumph quickly faded as her body registered its position.

Kyra lay beneath Lucy, with her wrists pinned either side of her head. Their lower bodies pressed together as Lucy pinned Kyra's hips down with her own. Lucy had felt the pull between them from the moment they had met; she had craved each and every touch, regardless of their innocent nature. Now though, her thoughts were far from innocent. Her eyes travelled down the toned body beneath hers. She watched as Kyra's chest heaved. She spied a tongue brush lips as she felt Kyra trying to bring her body under control. In that moment, that very moment she knew what it meant to be Doku. She could feel her nerves singing, as her bare skin brushed the skin of the woman beneath her. She could smell the most intoxicating scent she had ever experienced. It was a mixture of sweat, arousal and something that was unique to the woman beneath her.

On instinct Lucy rolled her hips into those beneath hers whilst she leant forward on her arms, bringing her lips to within an inch of Kyra's. She inhaled Kyra's scent and felt the actual moment were her eyes changed again bringing back the blue of her kind.

At Kyra's barely concealed moan, Lucy gave in and crashed their lips together. A shock-wave emanating from their lips travelled down Lucy's body where it settled between her legs and throbbed. Craving more contact Lucy rolled her hips again, this time with much more pressure and intent. Kyra arched her back in answer, trying to gain some sort of friction as they writhed together. Lucy lowered her mouth to place where Kyra's slender neck met strong shoulder. Her tongue crept out to taste the salty skin, and any last shred of restraint snapped. She released Kyra wrists, and quickly leant back so she could pull her hair free from the ponytail it was trapped in. Kyra wasted no time, she rose up to thread her fingers through her Lucy's golden hair and pull her back down.

Their mouths hungrily connected as both women lost themselves in each other. The battle for dominance quickly settled into a synchronized clinch. The passion rose again and the need for oxygen became apparent. Lucy pulled back and greedily gulped in air, watching as Kyra did the same. The dark haired woman's skin was flushed, covered in a thin sheen of sweat. To Lucy she had never looked more beautiful. She was hesitant to break the spell that covered them but she needed to know that Kyra felt the same. She licked her lips and looked straight into her eyes as she hesitantly asked

"Is this what you want?" Immediately Kyra raised herself to a seated position, holding onto Lucy's hips so she didn't jolt her from where she sat astride her. Without a single word she gently gripped Lucy's right wrist, bringing it to her lips as she softly kissed and nibbled her palm. Lucy forgot how to breathe as her middle and index fingers were sucked into the warm wet cavern of Kyra's mouth. In another flash of movement Lucy found the positions reversed as she felt her back firmly hit the Kiji mat below her. Kyra's beautiful face hovered over her as she knelt above her. It took a moment for her to register that Kyra was speaking. At her puzzled expression Kyra chuckled and lowered her lips to the shell of her ear.

"Focus. I said did you want an answer to your question?" Lucy nodded, not even being able to fathom how to try to speak. She could feel where her wrist was still in a firm grip, as it was being drawn down the body of the goddess above her. As the damp tips of her fingers reached the waistband of Kyra's board shorts she felt Kyra let go but the message was clear. She was wanted, THIS was wanted, but it was up to her to move forward. With no more hesitation she slipped her hand past the barrier of shorts and underwear to feel soft folds and silky wetness. She wasn't sure who growled and who moaned but the noises only spurred her on. She thrust two fingers into the woman above her, using her other hand to guide the movement of her hips. Kyra moved smoothly, riding Lucy's fingers in long movements so she could feel the woman fill her, touching her exactly where she needed her. As her climax built she craved even more contact. She fell forward, bracing herself on her arms. In a move so familiar it seems almost choreographed she pulled Lucy's mouth to hers, sighing as her tongue was instantly granted access. She rocked her hips firmer and Lucy answered by pushing her fingers even deeper, brushing the firm spot that pushed the strong woman over the edge. Lucy kept her fingers moving as firm muscles clenched around them, holding the digits tightly within her. As she came hard and fast, Kyra's moans were devoured by Lucy. Her fingers drew out every tremor and keening moan until Kyra's arms buckled. Mouth to mouth, with no space between them, the only sound in the room was the harsh breath of a woman trying to calm her raging body. The heat in the room was palpable as if the two women had in fact set fire to the air around them.

Lucy slowly withdrew her hand from within Kyra's heat and rested it gently on her own forehead. The moment she moved the scent of the arousal coating her fingers hit her like a truck. She became so very aware of the desire that was coating her own thighs. It was a pulsing reminder that her hunger had yet to be sated. Luckily Kyra was a perceptive woman, not that anyone could ignore the azure glow from the eyes of the woman beneath her. Her thin shorts didn't shield her from the heat that seemed to be blasting from Lucy's core. Sex should always be an enjoyable experience, but sex whilst in a Doku state was just so much... more. The smells, tastes and touches were all heightened, so much stronger and Kyra could not keep Lucy waiting a second longer. As Lucy pushed up, intending to kiss her again, Kyra gently placed a finger to Lucy's mouth. She raised her hands to indicate that she should wait as she rocked back to sit on her heels.

In one swift movement she pulled her tank top and bra upwards and threw it to the side of the room, quickly followed by her shorts and underwear. Lucy took in this new sight greedily. Kyra was indeed an incredibly beautiful woman. She looked stunning in whatever she wore, whether a cocktail dress or simple training gear. But like this, she was more than breathtaking. Lucy let her eyes travel down the skin she should see. Lines on the skin detailed the outline of firm, powerful muscles. Biceps, triceps and abs stood perfectly defined under shimmering skin. Her eyes were drawn to a simple black mark, a tattoo on Kyra's ample left breast. The mark resembled the writing found in the old books that Jonah poured over, day and night. Her hand rose of its own volition, a single finger brushing the outline of the symbol, not too dissimilar to a capital Y. Her curiosity got the better of her and she just had to ask.

"What does this mean?"

Her voice gave out low and husky, which seemed to amuse Kyra. She raised her eyebrow quizzically.

"Do you really want to talk about this now?" She watched as the blonde's eyebrows furrowed. Kyra crawled forward and placed her hands on the bottom on Lucy's sports bra.

"Because I was thinking we could continue with our physical activity?"

Lucy's curiosity immediately abated as her arousal made itself know again. Desire and hunger crawling under her skin as she raised her arms and felt herself be freed from her top. As soon as it was gone Kyra's mouth found its way home to Lucy's. Lucy caught a plump bottom lip between her teeth and pulled slightly, not enough to cause any real pain but enough to convey a message. The message was read loud and clear. Kyra shifted forward to press Lucy once again against the mat. When oxygen yet again became an issue she removed her mouth and began kissing her way down the sharp jaw, alternating between little nips, sharper bites and long firm tongue strokes. She continued down the centre of her chest, tasting the tangy salt skin as she went. Without warning she took a straining nipple into her mouth, enjoying the sound emitted as she rolled her tongue around the nub. Bringing her hand up, she palmed the other breast. Strong hips still clad in tracksuit bottoms rocked into her stomach. Her concentration broke, only to focus again on a new goal. She continues kissing her way down taut abs until she reached the waistband. She took one end of the drawstring lace between her perfect teeth and gently pulled, releasing the tie. She was immensely gratified to hear the sharp inhalation from above as hips again began to move. Looking up from under her lashes she saw the blonde with her hands fisted in her own hair, obviously trying to quell her arousal. Satisfied that she had teased enough she gently hooked her fingers into the waistband, amused when she found no underwear. With one quick pull and a helpful kick the bottoms joined the previously discard items that were strewn about the room. Kyra placed her hands on Lucy's ankles, and then ran her fingers on a path up the toned legs until she reached the knees. She pushed them apart opening Lucy up. She took the time to breathe and to gather herself. She shifted her own knees close together to support her as she leant forward, lifting both of Lucy's legs to rest over her shoulders. The move opened Lucy up even further, her clitoris peeking out from underneath its hood. Kyra closed her hands and yet again inhaled the scent around her. She slowly ran her tongue up the wet slit, delighting in the legs tightening around her neck. When she reached the clitoris she swirled her tongue around the engorged button before slowly taking it into her mouth to suckle. Thick wetness coated her mouth, tongue and chin. Lucy writhed beneath her trying to push herself further into the talented mouth that was devouring her.

Eager to please, Kyra shifted to thrust her tongue into the tight entrance and worked in and out at a blazing pace. Lucy arched her back, bracing her shoulders on the mat whilst clenching her thighs pushing the talented tongue even deeper still. A hand pressed itself to her abdomen, trying in vain to hold her still. Lucy was not prepared for the feeling that bubbled up from within her chest. It felt like a blazing ball of heat. The heat expanded into a throbbing mass and wrapped itself around every nerve and fibre of her being. When she had almost reached the crescendo of her pleasure, she felt two fingers twist into her core. She came hard and fast, the intensity of her orgasm shocking both herself and the woman beneath her. Her cry echoed off the wall, an almost primal sound that resonated back into her own ear drums.

8

Lucy had expected things to change dramatically after what had happened in the gym. It had been less than 24 hours ago since their shared intimacy in the gym had progressed into them seeking a bed, then turn into a repeat performance. The sex had been great, well amazing really and Lucy was sure that Kyra must feel something for her. But the dark haired woman had seemed to almost ignore Lucy since. She had been suspiciously absent from her bed when she awoke, and now she was late for breakfast. As was Jonah. Lucy quickly finished her toast and clad in her training gear made her way to the gym. It was empty yet it still managed to evoke a blush. Her quarters and the training areas were all housed beneath the ground level of the main estate building. She had been offered a tour, a fair few times but she had always declined. Instead wanting to remain focused she had kept her attention on her training. Maybe it was time she took a wander.

The large steel staircase wound up to a steel door, hidden behind a large bookcase in the main library. It held a hint of cliché but it worked. Clicking the case back into place, she heard raised voices coming from the left hand side of the building. She crossed silently to the door. She took a deep breath and reveled in the warmth of her power strumming its way through her extremities. Her hearing had shown improvement through training but she didn't really need it right now. She could make out Kyra, Jonah and an unknown woman having some sort of argument. The lack of sounds of breaking furniture quelled her rising fear. But she decided to try and remain stealthy anyway, she was curious after all. Suddenly Kyra's voice rang out.

"Mama I get it, believe me I do but I am a grown woman. I can make my own decisions."

Well that solves the mystery of who the visitor is.

"No Mija I don't think you do! The council has sent messengers everyday for you. They say they can't tell me anything because it is not any of my affair. With your father gone, they tell me nothing. I have no status. Why wont you tell me what you have done?" Jonah took that chance to join in once again.

"Madam, if I may. Your daughter's actions are completely honorable."

"Then why is it Dr Klein that when I look into her eyes I know that she is keeping something from me?" Jonah and Kyra seemed to flounder. Lucy felt guilty at being so much trouble. She had grown up without her mother, she wasn't going to cause a rift between Kyra and hers. Stepping out from behind the wall, Lucy summoned up every scrap of people skills she possessed.

"Hello Mrs Noble. I believe I am what, well *who* your daughter has been hiding."

Clara Noble was not easy to shock. After falling in love and having children with a man who was a lot more than he seemed had left her quite unshakeable. But seeing someone who was the spitting image of her late best friend stood in her old hallway rendered her speechless.

"Lucy? Is that you?" Lucy nodded, a little surprised that she had been recognised so easily. The withdrawal from the tea had led to several interesting dreams. Dreams that Kyra had confirmed were in fact memories. Memories that included tea parties and lake swimming, with a tiny Kyra. She could vaguely remember the woman in front of her. She remembered her with a few less lines but she was definitely the same woman.

"Yes it's me. I know this may be difficult to explain but.." She never got to finish her sentence as she was engulfed in a tight hug.

"Little Lucy you are ok! It's been so long. I am so sorry to hear about your Grandmother. Mona was such a wonderful woman, and please call me Marion." You could have heard a pin drop. The look of shock on Lucy's face was directly mirrored on Kyra's. Jonah seemed less surprised.

"What? You thought I didn't know? Kyra your father and I were married for over thirty years. We had no secrets from each other." Kyra had a face like thunder.

"So you knew all this time that she was alive?! I was 7 years old and I thought my best friend was dead!!"

No-one was prepared for her outburst; Kyra herself seemed a little taken aback. With barely a second look Kyra stomped towards the library. Lucy made a move to follow but was stopped by a hand on her arm. She was surprised it was Jonah.

"Lucy. Let me?"

He didn't wait for an answer before he headed in the direction that Kyra had gone. The two women remaining in the room shared an awkward look that spoke volumes.

"Well my dear why don't we take a seat and catch up because it seems there's a lot that we have both missed."

They both sat down on the plush sofa facing the window. Lucy shifted under Marion's studying gaze.

"Don't worry so much my dear. I will save the interrogation for my daughter when she has finished sulking. I only wish to know how you are." Lucy answered in a rush.

"Well that's quite a loaded question I suppose. 8 days ago I worked in a bank and now I receive daily combat training from a woman who could probably bench press a horse. I found out my parents were murdered and now I can make my eyes glow. That's pretty much how I am" Marion smirked.

"You have your mother's sense of humour. Sarcasm, wit and such a kind heart." Lucy's cheeks coloured a little with pride, before her eyebrows knitted in concern.

"Why did Kyra go off like that? I can understand her being angry but she doesn't seem angry at her father or Jonah for that matter and I'm pretty sure he knew too. I don't understand her." Marion took Lucy's hand before she spoke.

"My daughter is not as complicated as she seems, Lucy. She has told you I am human, yes? Well that makes her a hybrid, her brothers too. The Doku people can be a little... cruel at times. Certain people believe that the Doku should not have relationships with humans. When my husband befriended your father it meant a lot to us all. Your parents accepted me instantly and were always supportive. Kyra was only two years old when you were born. She was intensely strong minded and told us that she would take care of you. She didn't have many friends but she loved you so much. You were best friends. The night of the fire we had to move quickly, our priority was getting you and Mona out of harms way. Kyra heard us talking to the police, and she was devastated. I held her whilst she cried herself to sleep for many months, and in all honesty I don't think she ever really got over it."

"But when she was older couldn't you have told her?" Marion sighed and rubbed her temples.

"Ray and I discussed it many times. But we know our daughter. She wouldn't have stopped until she had found you and that would have painted a target on both your backs. We have never found out who killed your parents, Lucy. Or why. We were trying to keep you both safe."

Lucy could understand that. She only known Kyra for a little over a week but she could see how strong she was. She also noticed how protective she was of Lucy. Constantly asking her if she needed anything. Lucy realised she also felt protective of her. The idea of her crying herself to sleep, over her no less made her heart ache almost painfully. Marion continued,

"That is why she is angry. She understands the secret from her father, he was after all doing his duty, from me it must seem like a betrayal. Even as a child she hated showing any form of weakness. Kyra can hide her emotions well, most of the time. But never from me. Not her Mama. Even today I saw her look at you like she can't believe you're here."

"Well she's doing a great job of taking care of me. She gave me a choice at first. A new life with plenty of cash somewhere brand new. Obviously with my abilities suppressed. Or she could train me, with a crash course in history from Jonah and we could deal with whatever threat is out there together, whilst working out who killed our parents" The last sentence was a slip, she and Kyra had never discussed who knew of her fathers murder. A shadow passed over Marion's face, but she hid her emotion soon enough. Like mother like daughter it seemed.

"Do not worry. I know my Ray was taken from me. I knew as well that she would never stop until she brings whoever acted to justice. My twin boys, Alejandro and Cesar are only 19 years old. They believe it to be an accident and for now it must stay that way. They are in Iraq serving in the British Army. I know it is another lie but they do not have Kyra's brains god bless them. They think like warriors. Charging into the council and demanding answers and hurling accusations would not do anybody any good."

"I'm not even sure that Kyra has a plan, she hasn't shared any thing and we haven't done much but train."

"Kyra always has a plan my dear. Right now she's focused on you. And that is a good thing. She's missed you, and there's so much you need to learn." They smiled at each other. Marion clapped her hands and stood.

“Right I think the plan for this morning shall be tea, toast and you my girl filling me in on the past twenty years of your life!” As she headed off in the direction of the kitchen Lucy pondered what was taking place down stairs.

The conversation downstairs had been much more heated. Jonah had caught up with Kyra in the gym, lying on her back in the centre of the Kiji. He had known Kyra since she was three years old. He had trained her, educated her and despite his sometimes gruff disposition he knew he loved her as if she was kin. What he had told Lucy in the bank had been true; he had spent the last 6 years in Canada. He and Kyra had been working in the Noble research center in Vancouver. Its public image was chemical research when in fact it was a Doku medical research and rehabilitation center. He’d watched her help many Doku heal including small children, he had watched her care yet she always tried to keep it hidden. The past few days he’d seen such warmth and care from her. He was no fool, he knew something had happened between the two women the night before, could tell from Kyra’s demeanor this morning. She had already been up and training before he had even switched on the coffee machine. Usually he had to drag her out of her comfy bed with promises of breakfast foods and strong coffee.

He had always been a loyal employee. This meant knowing when to keep his opinions to himself, it was entirely possible this was one of those times but he could not keep silent. He eased himself down onto the mat beside the obviously brooding woman. He was no stranger to her moods.

“Maam, are you ok?” He was anticipating silence not the rant that followed.

“No I’m not alright. She knew! She KNEW! She let me cry for so long. We had a funeral! The little white coffin. Remember?” And remember he did. The service was awful but necessary to maintain the story. They had called in so many favours from Doku and Human alike. From fire officials to morgue attendants to keep the story ringing true. No funeral for Lucy and Mona would have been stupid. He nodded sagely.

"Jonah we buried her! And I cried for her. She was my best friend and it broke my heart to lose her. I was exactly a popular kid. No-one wanted to be my friend and she was. I'm not explaining this right." She huffed and sat up.

"I understand your anger. What I don't understand is why it is only directed at your mother? Your father and I kept the secret too. I patched Lucy up after the fire, Mona too. I drove them to their new home. I even prescribed the Blinken tea for Lucy."

"I know that. I just. I don't know. I think I just didn't want to admit that it hurt so much being the last to know."

"Kyra. You know now. She's here. She's not going anywhere and neither are you."

"Jonah we don't even have a plan. We don't even know how to find out who did this to her, who took my Dad. I need to know why! I can't think past wanting to rip someone apart!" He knew she'd been holding things in for a while. She hadn't even cried for her father yet, she kept saying she'd take the time to grieve after the funeral. Then it was after she'd gone through his things. Which had once again been sidelined, due to the reappearance of Lucy. He could tell she was close to breaking down, as she wiped angrily at her eyes.

"Which is why I am here. To do the thinking for you." He smiled warmly and Kyra sat up straight.

"You have a plan?"

"Oh yes."

"Care to share O wise one?" He grumbled at her sarcasm but continued.

"The council is convening in London in a month for the Dokain Games. Not only will the council be there but there will also be hundreds of our people. You are being instated in your father's seat and I propose that we add a little extra to the ceremony."

"You mean Lucy?" He nodded.

"How is that safe? We don't know who we're looking for!"

"You're right we don't, but we know that we are most likely looking at one of the larger families. The number of lackeys that came shows it had to be a larger family. They were mercenaries that much was obvious. They had an unaffiliated Doku insignia and they didn't identify themselves but we're very well trained. I'm not entirely sure they were Doku. That means someone doesn't want it traced back to them. That set-up takes money. Bringing Lucy out in a public domain in front of the entire council will be the quickest way to not only find our enemies but to also find our allies."

"You think that'll work?"

"It's our best shot. We can't hide Lucy here indefinitely. And we don't have the time to play Poirot with everyone one else. You are well respected, as was your father as was Lucy's. That gives us a foundation. And you have me by your side, as always."

Kyra leant her head on his shoulder and closed her eyes. The relief of having a plan in place felt amazing. Her next order of business was the juvenile way she had treated Lucy this morning. *Lucy. What the hell did she feel for her?* She had known her as a women for a week and she couldn't stop thinking about her. She'd bedded women before, both Doku and human but this felt completely different. It was too quick to be love. But she couldn't deny it was unlike anything she'd ever known

"We should go upstairs. I need to apologise to my Mama." Kyra jumped to her feet and jogged to the stairs. Jonah only a little way behind.

The sound of breaking glass startled them both.

9

Lucy and Marion had been having a lovely conversation, sharing stories and asking questions. That ground to a halt as the window in front of them shattered. Lucy's abilities no longer hampered came to the fore quicker than she had ever imagined.

The glass hadn't even hit the floor before Lucy had thrown herself over Marion. Shards landed in her hair and sliced her skin but she paid it no mind. Without thought she quickly grabbed the frightened woman and ushered her towards the library. They had just reached the door, as the sound of boots hitting the wooden floor resonated through the room. Lucy counted four pairs. She's not sure how she knew that, the sounds came barely a tenth of a second apart yet to her they were easily discernable. She urged the woman forward, into the library just as the bookcase clicked forward.

Kyra and Jonah's eyes were already aglow as they came through the door. Lucy thought it best to get to the point.

"Living room, four of them and since they used the window and not the doorbell I don't think their here to welcome me into the fold." Kyra looked at Jonah who wordlessly handed her a handgun. He handed another to Lucy. Kyra glanced her way.

"Lucy, take my Mother and lock yourselves downstairs." Lucy was having none of it but didn't get the chance to argue. Kyra pushed Marion through the door but couldn't reach Lucy before a shot rang out. Kicking the bookcase into place, she rolled to the left behind her father's desk.

"Mama! Lock it!" The sound of the bolts slamming into place at least assured her she'd keep one person safe.

Scanning the room she took note of everyone's position. Jonah was in the left corner of the room adjacent to the entrance while Lucy mirrored his position. Both had the safetys off and were ready.

Kyra could detect the slight quiver in Lucy's arms, but was impressed that she looked so comfortable with only a few hours weapons training. The seconds seemed to stretch as the wait was on for who would make the first move. Kyra was never known for her patience. They needed to draw fire to better ascertain the enemies' position. She held up her hand to signal to hold fire. Looking for something useful she spied her father's office chair. All it took was a hard kick and the chair went sailing across the floor. A sail of bullets tore through the chair but not before revealing the position of two assailants. Kyra fired off two shots, satisfied by the sound of a body slamming into the floor. Jonah chose to pull a knife from his boot and let it fly. The shot was silent, but the sickening thud of the knife meeting flesh. A nod from Jonah signaled the success of his aim. Lucy was breathing hard but maintained her focus. A streak of black reflected by the glass littered floor, drawing her attention. As she felt herself become anxious she reminded herself what was at stake. Who was at stake. Another streak hit her peripheral vision and she let off three shots, hearing only one hit its marks. No sound signaled the man hit the ground so she shook her head. A rolling clink interrupted proceedings, and soon the air was filling with smoke.

Lucy tried not to panic, she really did but they hadn't covered 'smoke filled room' protocol in their limited training. She began to shake. Falling apart now would not work. A slight creak behind her made her jump but somehow she knew it was Kyra. Kyra pressed herself up against Lucy's back and whispered in her ear.

"Focus Lucy. There's two left. One is injured. Remember who you are, who we are we are faster and stronger. They take our sight so we use everything else."

It wasn't the words that brought her comfort but the voice that delivered them. They remained pressed against the wall as random shots ricocheted through the room. It took a moment for Lucy to note that Kyra had angled her body in front of hers. She could not be a liability; she would not be the reason why anybody got hurt.

The smoke was cloying and burnt where it entered lungs, the three allies needed a moment. Just a single moment to end this. Jonah took the initiative and shot through the library window. The confusion at this action gave way to understanding as the room began to clear. The opening came from an overzealous assailant. He was definitely human and he had no idea who he was dealing with. He rushed forward, gun raised but he had no time to shoot. Kyra kicked the gun from his hand whilst keeping hers trained on his head. Lucy noted his side was bleeding, probably from her earlier shots. Working quickly Lucy struck his wounded side with her gun, bringing him to his knees. The kick to his face knocked him unconscious.

The last attacker remained quiet. Kyra signaled to Jonah that she was advancing forward. The sharp shake of his head was expected but Kyra repeated the signal. Suddenly a voice rang out from the right hand side of the hallway.

"We are here to deliver a message!" Kyra quirked an eyebrow in Jonah's direction before yelling back.

"Oh and who exactly is sending this message?"

"I am employed on behalf of The Crucible." Lucy whispered,

"Who's The Crucible?" Kyra and Jonah shared a look that easily translated into 'we have no idea'. Kyra raised her voice again.

"So you break into my house, rain bullets at me and attack my family to deliver a message? Better be fucking good mate! And I'm not sure if you've noticed but it's no longer a 'we' situation, you're on your own now."

Silence reigned until laughter filled the air.

"What makes you think its only us here?"

The alarm bells rang too late in their heads. They had had no chance to check their surroundings. The man had served his purpose to serve as a distraction, to draw their attention whilst a shot was being set. It was over too quickly. The moment of comprehension was punctuated by a bullet hitting its target. The damp spray of blood hit both women a second before Jonah hit the floor. Glass cracked as inside man vacated the home he had just helped to violate. Bullets from Kyra's gun followed him blindly as she pushed Lucy down out of the windows line of sight. She threw herself to Jonah, hoping her eyes were lying. It was not so. His eyes were lifeless, hair matted with blood and no hope of life. Kyra pulled him close, feeling her clothes dampen with blood. She heard screaming then realised it was her own throat making the sound.

Lucy could not move. He was gone. Before she was conscious of the movement her legs were pumping as she chased the man who had ran. She was out of the front door and across the front lawn in less than five seconds. She didn't shout. She gave no warning. She just fired until her gun was empty. The open air buzzed through her senses as she heard the distant whir of a helicopter. She sloped back into the manor, confronted with twin sets of sobbing. The library contained a mother holding her daughter who held yet another loss.

Turning to the main hall wall Lucy was confronted with a 6ft high image of the insignia worn by the bastards who did this. Underneath was scrawled the words:

LET THE GAMES BEGIN

Printed in Germany
by Amazon Distribution
GmbH, Leipzig